MW01241553

A Night
with you

WILLOW WINTERS

From *Wall Street Journal* Best Selling Author, Willow Winters comes a steamy, small-town romance.

Before I walked through those doors, I knew fate had something in store for me. It gave me chills, the good kind. My high school crush was standing behind that bar in our small town waiting for me to walk in and see him mixing up a cocktail I couldn't resist.

He glanced my way and a nervousness shot through me as if he never left.
Then he smiled that handsome charming grin I remember all too well and I knew I was in trouble. The kind of trouble that breaks a girl's heart but leaves lasting memories.

We aren't kids anymore though and I've always wondered if Bennet Thompson could kiss me like he did in my dreams… Now that he's back something tells me, tonight is going to be more than worth it.

This is book 3 of the Fall in Love Again series and can be read on its own although you'll want to read the others when you're done!

The Fall in Love Again series will feature Bennet and Bree falling in love on the small town fictional street of Cedar Lane over and over again while the real world has had other plans for them. Because love is endless and this is what forever means. In any and every life, their love was meant to be. And there's so much to tell in the dreams where they get to meet again for the first time every night.

A Night

with you

Prologue

Aubrey

I CAN'T HELP BUT SMILE AS THOSE FLUTTERING feelings go through me. The little butterflies that just won't quit whenever Bennet looks at me like that.

"Stop it," I mutter as I playfully bat his right arm. "Focus on driving," I tell him, grinning so hard my cheeks hurt and I'm certain they're bright red as well. His hand lands on my bare thigh and the rough pad of his thumb runs soothing circles against my heated skin.

His charming smile stays right where it is as he glances at me from the driver's seat of his truck and promises he's doing the best he can 'when you look like that'.

"If you wanted me to focus on anything other

than you, maybe you should have thought twice about that dress."

"Oh yeah," I play along, leaning closer to him and letting my hand fall on top of his. His touch does something to me I've never felt before.

"Yeah," he tells me, glancing again at me with those puppy dog eyes. "I love that color on you."

Love.

That little word has a ball of emotion swelling in my throat but I'm quick to swallow it down and I don't think my expression changed in the least. Staring straight ahead I ignore the one word I've been hoping he'd say and instead I tell him, "well next time I'll wear a paper bag."

He chuckles deep and rough and I love it.

Just like I love the way he makes me feel, I love every minute we spend together… I love his flannel shirt that he never buttons. I love the white tee underneath that's stretched tight over his broad shoulders. I love his tanned skin and the little grooves of his corded muscles, I love his jeans and the sound they make while he's kicking them off and making my bed groan as we get lost in the sheets every night.

I don't say what I want though when I glance back

at him at the red light before we get back to his place from a long night out.

He winces slightly and then rubs the back of his neck.

"You looking to get a massage?" I ask him playfully and then offer it up rather than tease and torment Bennet. "You could just ask," I tell him.

He chuckles again and then says it's just a little headache but he's more than happy to take me up on that offer.

Before the light turns green, I swear he's about to say something else... something that brings a shine to his eyes, but the damn thing interrupts us... just like everything else in the small town that was never prepared for a love like ours.

chapter
One

Aubrey

I CAN'T SHAKE THE NERVES FROM THE DAY NO matter what I do. For all intents and purposes, it was a wonderful meeting with the publishers, and the promotion to head editor is something I never expected. As I pull the high waisted floral skirt into place and adjust my white sleeve blouse so it's loosely tucked in, I know I love my job but I never expected this.

It's been a dream of mine for as long as I can remember. Today feels like so much more. Digging through my makeup bag, I settle on a deep rouge lipstick that will pair well with my heels.

My phone pings and I suppress my sigh and eye roll and opt for a grin instead. The girls are taking me out tonight to celebrate and I wonder if that's why I'm a bundle of nerves. It's been a long damn time since we've been out on the town and I know they're going to try to hook me up with someone.

And finding a guy, let alone hooking up with one, is not on my to do list.

The phone pings again on the sink countertop and I glance down at it.

The text reads: *You almost ready?*

Lauren is always ready early and she knows I'm almost always five minutes late.

I wouldn't be surprised if she walks across the street past her perfectly manicured rose bushes and knocks on my front door within the next two minutes.

Just as I pucker and smack my lips, there's a knock on the door and I nearly laugh out loud. I know it's not Lauren though when my front door opens.

"Bree!" I slip the lipstick into my clutch, snag my phone in my left hand, heels in the right. "Let's go!" Marlena and Gemma both call out.

"I'm coming!" My heart beats even faster on the trip through my house to the entryway, where my friends are checking themselves out in the mirror by the door. I laugh at Gemma blowing herself a kiss in the mirror. Her little red cotton sun dress is adorable. "We just need—"

The front door opens again, and Lauren steps in.

"You did it!" she shouts, and then I'm surrounded by a hug and squeals from my friends, all of them shrieking with happiness.

"Stop, stop, I'm going to get lipstick everywhere!"

My friends release me, laughing. Lauren rolls her eyes. "Please, Bree. You're perfect. I can't wait to get to the bar and show you off."

A shiver runs down my spine. "I don't need to be shown off, I just want to celebrate with you three."

Lauren cocks a brow and Gemma lets out a laugh before sharing a look with Marlena.

I hook my arm through Lauren's, my pulse coming quicker.

"Where are we going anyway?" I question and their answer is easy. The breeze moves through my hair on the way to Lauren's SUV. She's always DD. As the seatbelt clicks into place, I feel practically giddy. Maybe there's just something in the air. I'm excited about the promotion, of course, but I worked hard for it. As shocked as I was to get the title of Head Editor, it also seems to fit.

Who knows? Maybe it's *tonight* that's special. Maybe tonight is the night that I'm finally the person I've been working towards being, with nothing from the past holding me back. What is it that people say? It's the first day of the rest of my life.

The bar is lit up from the inside, practically beckoning us to the door. For a minute, as we get closer, it almost feels like high school again. The nights we went to football games and ate pizza at the little restaurant downtown were like magic. We felt like the world was just opening up for us, like anything could happen. Like anyone could walk through the door.

Though at the time, it wasn't just anyone I thought about.

It was someone very specific.

And tonight reminds me of him, even though it's a night out with the girls, and he moved across the country a long time ago.

I try to shake off the memories, and Lauren pulls me closer to her. "Cold?"

"Excited!"

She laughs. "Yeah, I bet! It's been way too long since we went out. Now that you're head editor, you'll have more time for us, right?"

"I'm pretty sure it's the other way around."

"No, no!" Gemma says. "You're the boss. You get to set your own schedule. That means you *have* to let us steal you away for wine down Wednesdays again."

"She's right," Marlena agrees. "You have to. Or else one day you'll turn around and realize you missed everything."

"Shh," scolds Lauren. "Bree's been here for everything. All the important stuff. Nothing else matters."

I make a silent promise to myself that I *will* spend more time with my friends. More responsibility at work doesn't mean I can let friendships fall by the wayside. I'm not willing to let any of them get away, not after—

Gemma pulls the front door of the bar open. Noise pours out onto the sidewalk. People talk over one another, music plays, and glasses clink.

"Drinks!" Lauren says over the noise, and pulls me with her toward the bar. A couple attached to each other at the lips veers into our path, and Lauren shoos them out of the way. The man's taller, and the woman has her hands in his shirt, and the way they're kissing is so intense that I don't see him at first.

But then my heart stops and my entire body freezes.

Bennet Thompson.

He stands behind the bar, tall and handsome just like he was in high school, his hands moving confidently on a glass and bottles while he mixes a drink.

My heart does a loop in my chest and straight up to my throat. I've thought about Bennet Thompson at least a few times a week since I graduated.

That's what happens when you have a crush on somebody. A crush is different from other kinds of love. It hides in your heart and pops up when you least expect it. Refusing to just go away because it was never even given a chance.

My whole face heats as Lauren pulls us toward the bar. I had no business having a crush on Bennet in high school, because he was dating Pamela. I have no business feeling this giddy at the sight of him now, but what am I supposed to say? I can't tell Lauren to stop, and more importantly I don't want to. I can't believe he's back in town.

I want to see him up close.

Oh, God, he's even more attractive up close. How is he hotter than my memories of him that kept me up at night?

He slides the glass across the bar to the woman it's for, brushes off his hands, and looks up.

Our eyes meet.

It's the first time I've looked him in the eyes since he moved across the country and the shock is no less powerful than it was all those years ago. The pale blue of his eyes lights up, and a slow smile spreads across his face. That's the smile of a heartbreaker, right there.

And oh, my heart is going to break. Because just looking at him makes me feel like I'd do anything to be near him, anything to see that smile again.

I'm in trouble.

Huge trouble. The kind of trouble that'll shatter my heart. I just know it. I'll be left with nothing but memories.

A wiser person might turn away and forget Bennet Thompson.

I smile back at him instead.

chapter
Two

Bennet

A T FIRST, I THINK I HAVE TO BE IMAGINING her.

Aubrey Peters, with her doe eyes staring straight at me and her beautiful red lips parted just slightly, proving she's just as shocked to see me as I am to see her. All I've got on is worn blue jeans and a white tee, and this gorgeous woman's little black dress and red heels put her way above my league.

There's no way Aubrey Peters is standing in my bar. Or—the one I work at since Steve let me bartend until I get settled back in town. There's no way she's standing there with her arm hooked through her friend's, looking at me with a beautiful blush spreading over her cheeks, exactly the way she used to look at me in school.

It takes great effort not to show every emotion on my face and keep my cool. Her friend—Lauren—says something to her, and the two of them come closer.

She's real. Aubrey is standing there, right in front of me, making my heart race all over again. The bar lights shine down on her hair and men on the other side of the bar turn to check her out, and I'm not surprised by the flare of jealousy straight through my chest. She and Lauren are at the bar in a matter of steps. I lean over to take their order, and I swear there's a magnetic pull between us.

"Hi," Aubrey says. I only half-hear the order Lauren places. My hands move automatically to make the drinks, and suddenly Lauren's gone. It's just Aubrey, leaning in too, her face lit up with surprise. "I didn't know you were back in town."

"I am." I open my arms and gesture at the bar. "This is what I do now."

"Flirt with women?"

I give her wide eyes. "Is that what it looks like I'm doing?"

"You're smiling a lot."

I can't help myself as she sways back and forth in front of me, "I'm smiling at you."

Even though half the ice completely misses the

glass, I keep going on the drinks as if I'm not hot and bothered. Aubrey laughs, tossing her hair over her shoulder, and I want to run my fingers through it. I want it so much I could jump over the bar and capture her in my arms, but I don't. I have more self-control than that.

I've been back for nearly two weeks now, working at the bar all week, and I haven't heard anything about her other than she's settled down in Cedar Lane. Although a quick glance at her finger tells me my definition of 'settled down' might be different from what I thought before.

"What have you been up to lately? You come here a lot?"

She grins, her eyes twinkling. "Working. I got a promotion, actually. That's why we're out tonight."

"A promotion?"

"Head Editor." Bree looks so damn proud of herself, and hell if I'm not proud, too. "I didn't realize they'd give it to me, honestly, but I'm thrilled they have."

"Drinks," I say, wanting to ask her a hundred questions about her new job. About her life since I've been gone.

But she picks up the tray I've pushed across the bar at her with a quick, soft *thanks*.

"It's good to see you," she says over her shoulder as she turns toward her friends and walks away.

I can't keep my eyes off her.

No matter how hard I try, I keep looking back at her table for the rest of the evening. Just being in the same room with her gives me a high like I haven't felt since I moved.

A few times, I catch her glancing at me. And each time I let an asymmetric grin slip into place.

The bar is busy and loud. People drink and enjoy themselves without stopping, but no matter how many orders I fill, I can't stop watching her. Nobody in this entire bar is as captivating as this woman, and my heart beats fast just to be in the same room as her.

How did I manage to stay away all this time? The memories flash by, college, a start up company and then selling it before being convinced to come back home for family... life is a wild ride but I never expected it to bring me back to her.

It's toward the end of the night when she comes back to the bar, her eyes bright from a night of drinking. She's confident and beautiful and leans right in.

"I wanted to say goodbye before I left," she said.

"Just goodbye?"

She bites at her lip, giving me a little grin that drives me wild. "I don't know. They've redone the bar since I came last. You could…" Her voice goes low with suggestion. "Show me the back… I heard there's a game room now or something?" One of her friends calls her name. "Just a second," she says back, her eyes hot on mine.

"It's this way." I play it cool on my way out from behind the bar. I know Steve is working on an expansion, but honestly I just wanted a job to keep me busy and to get back into the swing of things. I tell her, leading the way, "It's different from how I remember it, but it's nice."

The narrow hall in the back pushes us close together, and Aubrey leans into it a little, her elbow brushing mine.

"Supply closet." I point at one of the doors. "And then back here is where the pool table will go I think, and a little more space for storage."

The space is barren, drywalled and the ceiling is all beams and HVAC systems. "It's not much to look at but it will be nice I think."

I flick the light switch but they don't turn on. "Not quite ready yet," I comment and then glance behind me, knowing full well the bar is waiting with the faded chatter just barely slipping through.

"Oh." Aubrey steps closer, her lips pursed, looking at the space. She makes a slow turn, her eyes traveling over everything, not moving away an inch. "You're right. It *is* nice."

"You're nice."

"You're not too bad yourself."

She tilts her face up, just a little, and I take that as a sign that I should kiss her. There's no holding back, now that we're alone in this shadowy back room, nobody watching.

My hands go to her face like we were never apart. Aubrey's eyes flutter closed, and then my mouth is on hers.

Bree's lips are just how I always thought they would be. Soft and sweet, tasting like the last cocktails I made. She dives right into the kiss, her hands going around my neck, and I back her carefully against the wall. Those soft curves. The feel of her. I can't think of anything else.

Somebody moans... not one of us and it's someone in the office.

My brow rises as the both of us look up and to the doorway.

The sound echoes out of a nearby background, and Aubrey puts her hand to her mouth and laughs. "Oh my god. We weren't the only ones with this idea."

A smile widens on my face as I look down at her. I brush her hair away from her face, unable to stop myself from laughing, too. "Well, it was a good idea I think. Come on. We'll go out this way."

Aubrey takes her phone out as soon as we step outside behind the bar, looking a little rumpled and sweet. "My friends are looking for me."

"You better go find them."

She sways slightly and I wonder what she's thinking.

"I'm glad you came out tonight Bree," I tell her and she grins like there's some secret only she knows. "Even more glad you wanted to see the backroom," I joke, running my hand through my hair.

Her teeth sink into her bottom lip and she nods before saying, "Same. I'm so glad I got to see you. Maybe I'll see you again?"

"Damn right you will," I tell her and then glance back to the bar, knowing it's waiting on me.

She smiles although her eyes hold so many questions, and I'll be damned if my heart doesn't skip a beat. "How about one more good night kiss?"

I lean down and kiss her, softer than before, and she laughs into it. The sound fills me with something like heat, something like joy, and I'm not going to get too far ahead of myself, no matter how right this feels.

Aubrey pulls back, the wind rustling her hair. "God, that was—that was nice. I have to go."

She whirls away, leaving me behind, and I lean against the back wall of the bar with a smirk spreading across my face.

This time, it doesn't seem so permanent to let her walk away.

Aubrey glances back at me just before she turns the corner and gives me a little wave. Then she's gone.

There goes my dream girl, giving me a memory and a view of her I'll hold onto forever.

chapter
Three

Aubrey

WITH MY EYES HEAVY AND A SLIGHT hangover, I wake up slowly, images from my dreams hanging on until the last possible second. Bennet Thompson was the star of all of them. I can't remember exactly what we were supposed to be doing in the dream, but I can remember what we did instead.

I remember the heat of his hands on my body and his mouth capturing mine and how perfect it was to be so close to him, like we were always meant to kiss like that.

In the dream, the lighting was dim, the way it was in the back of the bar in that room under construction. I kept expecting for someone to walk in on us—I think I could hear voices—but nobody did. And there was nobody else moaning in the dream. It was just the two of us, and Bennet seemed as absorbed with me as I was with him.

It felt so vivid, like it wasn't just a dream. Almost like we'd been dropped into another life and found each other there. Even in my dream-life, I guess my main priority is to make out with him in a darkened room.

In my dream life, he was an amazing kisser… just like he is in real life.

I flip my pillow to the cool side and stretch, but it doesn't do anything to get rid of the electric sensation of needing more.

Smiling into the pillow, it's almost embarrassing how much I want him. I still can't believe I kissed him. I almost did it out there in front of everyone. A quick peck and then run off. But I wanted to make sure I wasn't making it up in my head and that he really wanted me.

I squeal into my pillow, reliving that memory from last night.

It's been a long time since I felt this needy over a man. I might've felt this way back in school, but I don't think I had the words—or the courage to kiss him, to be honest.

Now I do.

Now I've done it, and it feels like my entire life is starting. A promotion. Bennet back in town. I know my life has technically been happening all along— I've worked hard for it—but something about this morning feels fresh and new and a little headachey.

I had a bit too much to drink last night.

How much *did* I have to drink last night?

My phone buzzes on the table next to my bed, and I pick it up lazily and hold it in front of my face.

There are *tons* of messages.

Another one comes in as I'm scrolling through them. It's from Gemma, sent to our group chat. My heart speeds up as the words sink in.

Did you two hook up last night?? Bree, answer us!

One from Marlena pops up just below that.

If they did hook up, he's a five-minute kind of guy.

There's no way, Gemma answers.

I hold shaking fingers over the screen and type out my own message. This isn't a dream, that's for sure. It's real sunlight streaming in through my bedroom window and real messages pouring onto my cell phone's screen. I glance at the clock reading nearly 9 am as my fingers fly across my phone and I type out a response.

Wait—did he tell people we hooked up?? I'm just now seeing all these, I slept in!!

Gemma sends five winking emojis, and then she's typing something else. I hold my breath and wait for the message to arrive.

He said you kissed but nothing else.

Good, I write back, adrenaline surging through my body. *I just woke up.* There hasn't been time for me to tell anybody anything, and now Bennet's put out a press release about the kiss we shared? I don't know whether to be embarrassed or excited or both.

There's nothing like living in a small town. The gossip has a way of bringing things to life that never should have existed. As if a small kiss between the two of us could ever be a scandal.

Good why? Marlena writes.

Because that's what happened

I leave it at that, fresh warmth spreading all over my face.

Gemma sends another text: *You made out with Bennet last night?!?!*

My front door opens downstairs, and this is it— this is when I talk about Bennet with my best friend in the entire world. If that doesn't make last night real and life-changing, I don't know what does.

"Aubrey Lynn Peters," yells Lauren.

It feels like the entire world has crowded into my bedroom. I know it's just my friends, but part of me thought that last night had been…subtle. That maybe nobody had noticed. That Bennet and I had been in our own little world.

That couldn't be farther from the truth. They *all* noticed. And then he went and told people, and I don't know what that means. Is he trying to play it off like it was no big deal, or is he telling people out of the same kind of excitement that I feel?

My face goes hot, and I burrow into my sheets and blankets as footsteps climb the stairs. A few seconds later, my bedroom door creaks as it opens wide.

"I know you're in here," Lauren scolds. "I can see you under the covers. Oh my God, Bree!"

I peek out from the blankets and find her smiling, her eyes wide and shocked at the same time. I've spent the last few years throwing myself into work and not spending nearly enough time with my friends, and now, on our first night out, I kissed a guy in the back room of the bar. No wonder she finds it surprising.

Lauren crosses her arms over her chest and shakes her head. "You don't waste any time, do you?"

"I guess not." I pull the blankets back up and

hide in them for another few seconds until it gets too warm. "The town is saying we hooked up last night? As in—*hooked up* hooked up?"

"Well, *someone* did last night." Lauren raises her eyebrows. "The town is saying it's the two of you."

My heart stops dead in its tracks. "We didn't do *that* last night."

"If it wasn't you and Bennet, then who was it?"

chapter
Four

Bennet

I PICK UP ANOTHER GLASS OUT OF THE RACK behind the bar and wipe it down, watching Steve drop his face into his hands across from me. He looks tired, the way he always does—the man owns a bar, and he doesn't get much sleep even when things are good.

Hell, *I* didn't get any sleep last night, for almost the same reasons he didn't, which he's just spilled to me over a pot of coffee.

"Steve." He looks at me from over his hands. "You've got to be kidding me."

"Look." Steve lets out a heavy sigh. "No one can know. I'm serious."

"Nobody can know you kissed your wife last night?"

He grimaces. "She's not my wife."

"You're separated, not divorced."

"I know that, but she said before—"

"I'm pretty sure she's changed her mind if she kissed you last night."

"She doesn't want anyone to know," he insists. "Everything is so damn complicated right now."

I put the glass in its place and pick up another one. "But?"

"But I felt it." He lets his hands fall onto the bar, palms up. "Sparks. Whatever you want to call them. I felt it when she came into the office last night. It's not over between us and I can't let some gossip and busy bodies get between us. I need to make this right with her."

"So you want me to take the fall for kissing *your* wife?"

"We're separated," he repeats back to me. "It wouldn't be the end of the world if—you know…" he trails off. The poor guy is stuck between a rock and a hard spot. "If the town thought it was you and Bree and they stayed out of our business…"

Steve looks desperate, and I feel for him.

I just…

I can't agree to this. The town talking about Bree

and spreading gossip that I don't think she'd be comfortable with … it's not just me who would have to agree.

Steve's right about one thing. It *is* complicated. He's the one who offered me the job and helped move me back to town. I owe him for that at the very least. I don't want to let him down and I know he still loves his wife. And I know how this town can be. But what I feel for Bree is real and I can't risk hurting the only chance I might ever have with her.

If it were anything else within reason, I'd be the first in line to help him.

"I don't do hookups in the back of bars," I tell him.

"Bennet, it's not like your boss is going to fire you."

I shoot him a look. "Isn't that a safety hazard, anyway?"

"I was in the office, for fuck's sake." Steve's phone lights up on the bar, and he checks it with a nervous twitch in his hands. "I'm afraid it'll be too much for her if the town starts talking and puts two and two together. You know how people like to play detective and give their opinion on everything. I've messed up Bennet. Putting this bar before her. Working our lives away and not being there for her when I should have been. She wants to give it another shot but without the judgment and all that shit."

It's harder to have trouble in your marriage when you know that everybody and their brother is going to be gossiping. I don't know everything about Steve's marriage, but I have to imagine the stress of the bar and a small business could weigh on anyone. I feel bad for Steve. I really do. If he has a chance with his wife, then I want that for him, but it's not Steve and his wife everybody will be talking about.

It's Aubrey.

And there is just no way I'm doing that to her.

I can't. I won't.

"I'm sorry, Steve." I look him dead in the eyes. "I can't lie; you know I'm a bad liar."

"No, no—you don't have to lie. Just don't say anything."

I huff and look away, not liking any of this. A lie of omission is as good as the real thing. I'm not going to lie about Aubrey, even through keeping my mouth shut. Protectiveness shoots across my chest like fire, which only makes me empathize harder with Steve. He's trying to protect his wife, too, but he's going to have to find another way.

"If it was just me, then fine. I don't care. But Aubrey was with me last night."

"Bree isn't even interested in dating. They'd never believe it and if they did, hell, they'd probably be happy she was getting some action."

A flare of disbelief and even a hint of anger run through me. People would run away with that rumor about Bree. They'd never shut up about it. He needs to be more careful with what he says, or—

Or what? One kiss doesn't mean *I'm* dating Aubrey. I inhale a deep breath and steady myself. It doesn't mean I have any claim on her. I can't shut Steve down right now, or he'll think I've lost my mind.

Blowing up at Steve over an off-handed comment, as much as I hate it, would probably get around town, too, and it would have the same result. People would talk about Aubrey. They'd make all kinds of assumptions about her private life, and nobody needs to be doing that.

Not when she's—

Mine.

It sounds clear in my head. Right. *She's mine.* I know she's not. I know that whatever was between us last night, it doesn't mean I can speak for her in the light of day.

The best move is to keep things focused on Steve and his wife, because that's what this is about. Not me and Aubrey.

I dry off another glass. "You need to come clean, Steve. That's the only thing there is to do. If you and your wife want privacy, you can ask for it. But I can't let people think Aubrey and I slept together when we didn't."

Steve runs his hand over his face and leans back in his barstool. It creaks behind him, and I wonder when the last time it was that he had a full night off. Maybe if he had more time to spend with his wife, they wouldn't be in any kind of situation right now.

"I know, I know. I'm sorry." He pauses with his hand still over his eyes. "Wait...Bree?"

"No, wait." Steve uncovers his eyes and looks me over. He leans closer, his eyes narrowed, and I know he's about a second from figuring out what happened between us. Shit, shit, shit. I never should have said anything. I should have kept her out of it. "Did something else—"

"Steve—"

"Did something else happen last night other than me falling back in love with my ex?"

Steve's eyes are bright, and he pushes his fingers

into the bar like a detective on one of those cop shows who's just been handed a major clue. "You and Bree? You and her are a real thing?"

It's like he just now realized what half the town already knows. I can tell he's happy for me, even if he thinks his world is going to crumble because this town doesn't shut up and his marriage is at the mercy of rumors and late nights.

I don't know what to say. I open my mouth to answer him, because he's sitting right there and I can't ignore the question, but I have no idea how to explain what happened last night without making things harder for Aubrey.

Just then, there's a sound up front—the latch on the door clicking into place.

Then the door swings open, and I can't say a thing because she's standing right in front of us.

chapter
Five

Aubrey

I DON'T KNOW WHAT I EXPECTED WHEN I GOT in my car and drove over here, but it wasn't the awkward silence that falls when I push open the door of the bar and step inside.

Bennet looks at me, his eyes wide, like he's surprised to see me, which is justifiable. And Steve—the man who has owned this bar for as long as I can remember—looks at me with a strange expression I can't pinpoint. The music is off. It's so quiet I can hear my own heartbeat.

"Hi." My voice sounds too loud without all the chatter of other people and the constant music that played last night, along with the game on the TV behind the bar, and my face heats up all over again.

This is the tenth time today. "I know you're not open, Steve, but if I could just…"

I motion to Bennet, who's wiping down the glasses behind the bar.

"Of course." Steve waves me over to the barstool next to him, rearranging his face. A little alarm goes off in the back of my mind, but I could be reading too much into it. Also, my heart is going a million miles an hour. "Good to see you, Aubrey."

"Good to see you, too."

This time, there's nobody else. I'm front and center. No distractions, no friends, nothing but the two of us. And no liquid courage. My heart flutters. At the center of that feeling is a warm spark that's pure excitement.

I'm not going to beat around the bush. "Did you hear the rumors?"

Steve frowns. "Did you want me to step out?"

"It doesn't matter." I look back at Bennet. He seems shocked, and his hands are in the air, the glass he was drying abandoned on the counter. "I wanted to ask you."

"I swear, Bree, I'm setting the record straight—" Bennet starts.

"No one believes it, Bree. Don't pay them any

mind," Steve says. He glances over at Bennet, and they share a look. Okay—something's definitely off, like the way he frowned, but I can't put the pieces together when my heart is pounding.

Bennet lowers his hands, placing them flat on the bar. "I hope you're not thinking last night was a mistake."

I steel myself and pretend it's just the two of us.

"Last night was wonderful for me, Bennet, but I don't want anyone thinking anything else happened unless..."

"Unless what?" Steve interrupts.

Bennet sighs and then scowls at Steve, "Maybe you should head to the back and do some inventory or something."

Stew swallows hard, the color draining from his face. He looks *panicked*. Is that why everything feels so off?

"Are you okay, Steve?" I ask, because if he's having some kind of emergency...if something's going *on* here...

"It's just, you know...it's not—it's like this, I—" He grips his coffee cup like it's a lifeline. "Hey, Bree, could I ask you a favor?"

Bennet looks his friend over. "I'm telling you it's

going to be fine. The truth is always the best way to go."

"I can't lose her again," Steve murmurs, softly and with so much concern, and my heart sinks.

"What's going on?" I ask, keeping my voice as quiet as his.

Steve looks me in the eye, a flush spreading across his face. "It was me and Sarah last night. In the back. We were—" He shakes his head. "She doesn't know what to think of it all, but she doesn't want the town prying into our marriage again."

I let out a breath.

"Oh my god."

I was as surprised as anyone to hear that Steve and Sarah, who were high school sweethearts, were on the rocks. But I also heard about how stressful it had become to run the bar. A remodel earlier this year had tons of delays, which meant the bar was closed for longer than they wanted. On top of that, Sarah had been through some tough times with her family. My heart aches for them.

"Please," Steve pleads with me and I don't understand.

"Please what?"

"Let them think it was you two," he asks and just

as his request registers, he hurries out more words, "I know it's a shitty ask and I know town gossip can be awful, but I'm begging you. I just want my wife to love me again and to work on our marriage in private."

I look away from him and at Bennet, whose eyes move between me and Steve, his mouth pressed into a thin line.

Holy shit. That was not at all what I was expecting.

"Either way Bree, if you say no, I'll respect it," Steve tells me and I look back at him, knowing full well that I don't care about town gossip in the least, but I know it played a part in what happened with Steve and his wife.

"I'm not a good liar," I start and the hope in Steve's eyes dim until I add, "I guess if you took me out to dinner tonight…" Bennet raises his eyebrows at my suggestion. "We wouldn't have to confirm anything, but we also don't have to deny anything?"

Our gazes lock. It feels like last night, only hotter, only more energy between us, and that kiss plays again in my memory.

Bennet cocks a smile.

"The Bree I remember was a good girl with a good reputation," he points out, his voice at a low, sultry pitch.

"*This* Bree cares less about what the town is talking about and more about whether or not you want to go out with me."

Steve lets out a 'thank you Bree', and I give him my biggest, brightest smile.

"This town loves to talk," Bennet counters.

"Yeah, they do," I agree. "We could give them something to talk about."

His smile turns hotter, though no less charming than I remember from school, and last night, and my dreams.

"Would you like that?" he questions, and then it really is like we're the only two people in the room. The heat in his eyes says we *could* be in a private room in a matter of minutes, and it would be just like the dreams I had last night. That heat rushes down my body from my face to my toes, and my skin actually aches for him to touch me again. I'd like it if we had more time, hours and hours...

"I think I would," I tell him.

Steve exhales and immediately picks up his phone off the bar and starts tapping at it, his fingers flying. I imagine he's telling his wife she doesn't have to worry.

Steve says matter of factly, even with a hint of emotion still in his tone. "Well, that settles it. Bennet, you're taking Aubrey out to dinner." Poor guy doesn't seem like he slept last night.

Bennet gives him a look. "I have my shift tonight."

"No, you don't." Steve looks up from his phone, relief clear on his face, then gets up from the barstool and makes a beeline for the back. "You officially have the night off," he calls over his shoulder.

I watch him go, hoping with all my heart that he and Sarah will be able to work things out. I want both of them to be okay

"So," Bennet says, drawing my attention back to him. His eyes travel slowly over my face, and I could swear I feel heat wherever his gaze touches my skin. I'm already craving more of it. I want to be on the other side of the bar with him, in his arms, but for now I'll let him look at me just like this. "I'll pick you up tonight, then? At…five?"

I smile back at him, feeling my face settle into an expression that's more *want* than *grin*. "It's a date."

chapter
Six

Bennet

STEVE DIDN'T JUST GIVE ME THE NIGHT OFF from the bar. He let me borrow his truck, too, since I don't have a vehicle of my own quite yet. I didn't need one in the city, and I haven't had time to find one, and...

All this is a distraction from my nervousness.

I couldn't figure out what the hell to wear or where to go. I'm more nervous for this date than I've ever been for anything else in all my life. My heart has been practically jumping out of my chest since Aubrey walked out of the bar earlier today.

If I'm honest, it's been causing a ruckus in my chest since I saw her last night. I couldn't sleep, thinking of her. I thought of a hundred different scenarios for how we might meet again since I didn't ask for her number. What I'd say if she showed up at the bar with her friends. What I'd say if we ran into each other at the grocery store. What I'd say if I went to her house and knocked on the door and told her I wanted a repeat of what happened at the bar.

In the end, none of them happened, because she walked into the bar, sat down across from me, and stole my heart.

If I'm honest...

I think she stole it a long time ago. I'm not sure why it took so long for me to notice, but that's the only explanation for how I feel about this date. Almost like it's already happened, and we're just catching up to how things are supposed to be.

I blow out a breath and try my damndest not to get ahead of myself.

I just want tonight to be perfect. That's what this is.

I can't even bring myself to mind that Steve and Sarah are in over their heads, because in a way, they gave us a nudge. Steve looked so pathetic sitting across the bar from me that it's no wonder Aubrey agreed to a date.

Though...

She didn't look like she needed much

encouragement. If Steve hadn't been there, we might have ended up having the same conversation.

And I'd have ended up here, behind the wheel of the truck in my own driveway, losing my shit over a first date.

My phone pings.

It's a text from my dad. I unhook my hands from the wheel and pick up the phone to read it.

Dad: *So, Aubrey Peters and you? You better be treating that girl right.*

Word really does travel fast in a small town. I roll my eyes. What I do with Aubrey is none of anybody's business. I drop the phone back into my cupholder and ignore the text. Damn, this town is something else. I loved growing up in a small town, but I had to leave after high school.

Partly because there was one girl I couldn't stop thinking about. Days. Nights. Weeks. Months. Years. I thought about her constantly. And back then Aubrey never looked twice at me. After all, I had dated one of her good friends and broke her heart. Aubrey never knew but it was because I couldn't stop thinking of her. It wasn't right to her friend, who's long gone and living her happily ever after on the other side of the country.

My phone pings again.

Dad: *P.S. I heard she likes peonies. Heard it from Dale at the flower shop.*

I pause, cocking my head and deciding small town gossip is good for something after all.

Okay. I have one stop to make before I pick up Aubrey. Good thing I got ready way too early, so there's plenty of extra time.

The flower shop isn't too far away from the bar. It's a little white storefront with three parking spots in front. I pull in less than five minutes later and jump out of the truck, my muscles aching like I've been sitting for days.

It's only been fifteen minutes, tops, but I'm so wound up about this date that I feel like I've been trapped in a chair for a day's worth of classes or meetings or *anything* that keeps me away from Aubrey.

The bells above the door chime as I go into the flower shop. It's crowded with plants in different arrangements. I make my way around them to the counter in the back, where Dale is waiting with his wife.

The guy looks way too casual. His glasses perch on his dark hair, and he peers down at the cash register with a careful look on his face, like he's trying to hide that my dad clearly talked to him about me. His wife stands at his side, beaming. She's not doing a damn thing to hide how excited she is. As I get closer, she nudges Dale with her elbow.

He does the fakest startle I've ever seen and clears his throat. "Bennet! What can I get for you?"

"Mind if I take a look at your bouquets?"

I'm already halfway around the counter, headed for the cold room where they keep the pre-made bouquets, expecting that Dale will wave me through.

"Bennet, wait."

I turn back, and his wife is standing there with a gorgeous bouquet in her hands. Peonies in pastel colors burst from the top. It's better than anything I could have picked out in the back, and it's clearly been made just for Aubrey.

"I just made this one," she says and before I can say anything the bell chimes again, taking my attention back to the front door.

A woman steps into the flower shop, pushing a lock of hair out of her face. She looks vaguely familiar, a bit older, but I'm not sure why I recognize her. Half of this town is like that. I can't place her so I look back at the flowers. Dale's wife has them all ready for me, tied with a ribbon.

"I think I'll go ahead and take those off your hands," I tell her.

I take a few steps forward and get my wallet out of my pocket, then hand over my card. Dale plucks it out of my hand and runs it, his wife still grinning about the flowers, and I can't wait to see Aubrey's face when I give them to her—even if my dad is a busy-body, along with everybody else in this town.

I guess sometimes it pays off, though I'll never admit that to my dad.

Dale hands me my card back, and then his wife gives me the bouquet. It has a decent weight in my arm. The scent of peonies is perfect. Near the door, the woman has stopped doing whatever it was she was doing with her purse, and our eyes meet again when she's about halfway through the flower shop.

She stops dead, her eyes going wide, surprise transforming her face. "Bennet? Is that you?"

It takes me a moment to realize I do know her. "Mrs. Baker," I lament as it hits me. She's a teacher from my high school, looking just a bit older with slight wrinkles around her eyes.

"How are you doing?" she questions with a wide smile but before I can answer she says, "I heard you were back in town."

My eyebrow shoots up, likely to my forehead, "You did, did you?" I've only been back a week and I'm barely moved in. "I'm still waiting on a few boxes but mostly back."

"I heard you came back to town for a reason," she peers down at the flowers in my hands and makes a little face like she's in on the secret. "I'm so happy you're doing well," she tells me and then brightens, "you two have fun."

Words escape me as I turn and watch Mrs. Baker, in all her glory, smug as can be, gather up a bunch of carnations and shoo me on.

I swear, this town's memory is as long as the summer days.

chapter
Seven

Aubrey

MY STREET HAS NEVER BEEN MORE captivating than when I'm waiting for Bennet to park in front of my house. Although for a Saturday, it's uneventful apart from Miss Shaw gardening at the far end of the street.

I watch through the front window like the outdoors is a movie, watching the late-afternoon light come down on the street. It makes everything gold. The leaves rustling in the trees. A flag on the house across the street waving in the sun. Everything seems more beautiful, in deeper colors, and it's all because I can't wait for this date to start.

I shake out the nerves and check my reflection in the front room mirror when the minutes tick by.

Finally, a truck comes down the street and slows

in front of my house. It's Steve's truck, which means Steve must have been really desperate…or else he *really* wanted Bennet to be able to take me out.

Maybe it was both. It probably doesn't matter, in the end. From what I've gathered, between last night chatter and this morning messages from town gossip, Bennet sold a startup company for a decent penny and flew home for a family event but decided to stay.

Whether or not that's true though is something I aim to ask tonight. A quick kiss in the back of the bar was one thing, a date another.

I open it to reveal Bennet, who's dressed up from his bartending clothes. He wears slacks and a white button-down with the sleeves pulled up to his elbow, and I can't take it. He did that on purpose… showing off his forearms. How am I supposed to look at him all evening when he's this hot? It's hardly fair.

Bennet bites his lip, looking at me like he's thinking the same thing.

"Hi," I say.

In response he pulls a bouquet out from behind his back. Peonies. "Oh my gosh," I let out with genuine surprise. The bouquet paper crinkles as I happily accept the flowers. I inhale deeply, loving the fragrance.

"I love them," I tell him and then catch myself.

My heart races. I try to keep it casual as I invite him in so I can at least put the flowers in water. "They're beautiful, thank you," I tell him and keep it lighter. Lauren gave me one rule and it was not to use the "L" word. I've already blown it.

"I'm glad you like them," he says as I look up from the mason jar and find him staring down at me in my kitchen. My mind races and I can just imagine all the dirty things we could do on this very clean countertop.

As if reading my mind, he shakes his head, a grin lighting up his face. "Ready to go?"

"I am." I swallow thickly and let him lead the way.

Bennet waits while I lock up, then offers me his arm and escorts me to the truck. With my hand wrapped around his forearm, skin against skin, more of last night comes back to me. The stolen glances and blush that came to his cheeks when he saw me across the bar.

It's almost too good to be true. He reaches ahead of us to open the door for me. I hold his hand tight as I climb into the truck. Again there's this shock and pull and the idea that all of this must be a dream.

"What a gentleman," I say, holding his hand for a few seconds longer.

"I'm trying," he says, then squeezes my hand and lets go. The truck jostles slightly as he closes the door.

"You're doing a good job, in my book," I tell him through the open window and he grins before jogging around the truck and climbing behind the wheel.

"The flowers especially. Brownie points," I tell him with a grin although I can't look him in the eyes as I do.

Bennet flashes another smile at me, and my heart skips a beat. "I'll keep it up, then."

He drives us to a little restaurant downtown. There aren't many upscale places in a town this size, and this one's known as the 'date' restaurant.

"Oooh, you're going all out tonight," I remark and Bennet laughs.

"It's the least I can do to say thank you for what you're doing for Steve," he tells me and I wonder if that's really what he thinks this is.

"Don't forget," I tell him, "we're here to be seen." As if this date is only for Steve.

"You're right," he agrees, then hops out and comes around to my side of the truck to help me back out. "I will definitely be playing it up for the crowd," he says with an uncontained smile.

"I guess I'll play along too then," I tell him before

biting down on my smile to keep it from being a bit too much. It feels almost like a dare. Almost like the rules don't matter.

Bennet threads his fingers through mine on the way to the front door, giving me a wink as we go. The hostess looks between us, her eyebrows going up for a fraction of a second. I smile at her like I have no idea what's going on.

"Reservation for Thompson," Bennet says.

"Right this way." The hostess smiles even wider, then leads us to a table in the front windows of the restaurant. We're surrounded by glass on three sides. Anybody walking past can see that we're here on a date.

Bennet pulls my chair out for me. "This okay?" he murmurs.

"More than okay. This is the whole point, right?"

"Mmm," he says. That's not a *yes*. My heart speeds up again as he takes his seat across from me and spreads his napkin over his lap. "Now. A lot's changed since high school… mind catching me up."

"That's a lot to cover in one date," I tell him with a simper as I smooth my own napkin over my lap.

Bennet shrugs, like he'd actually sit here in this

restaurant until I'd told him absolutely everything about me. "Start at the beginning."

"I was born in town, went to school here…" I say jokingly.

"Oh, I remember that." His eyes light up. "But go on."

"I got into editing during college."

"You went to state right?" he asks and I nod, surprised he knew that.

"And when I saw the open job here, it just made sense to interview."

"Had enough of the city?"

"Yes." Memories resurface from my time away from town. "It wasn't bad. I had some really happy times in college. But I guess I just felt like I was meant to be here."

A waitress with a simple black shift dress leans in to fill our water glasses and take our orders, and we're off.

Over warm bread and butter, I tell Bennet about the first apartment I ever rented during senior year and how scary it felt to take out a mortgage to buy my house and how the first year of my job drained the hell out of me but at the same time was a dream come true.

"Did you always know you wanted to do that?" he asks, and for a few seconds I can't answer. I'm too taken with the shape of his lips and the carved lines of his face and the way his eyes linger on mine. There's that heat again, in every inch of me.

In that same moment, I feel other eyes on me and glance away from the table.

"I just don't remember you talking about editing or publishing back in high school."

It's not a big restaurant, and at least one person at all of the closest tables quickly looks away, pretending to be absorbed in their food.

"I…" I turn back to Bennet. "I always loved reading but I didn't realize I wanted a career in publishing until later."

He smirks as he catches me looking over my shoulder again.

He leans in, darting a glance out to the rest of the space. "They're all looking at us, aren't they?"

"Yeah. They're staring."

We share a barely heard laugh at the ridiculousness of this town before I get to ask him what happened when he left. Business school took up most of his time and it turns out the start up was wonderful, the payout was even better and helped his parents get out of debt, but he found himself alone afterwards not knowing what to do. The conversation moves easily enough and the dishes come and go leaving us with nothing but drinks and laughter and more and more questions. Several times we were interrupted by old neighbors and classmates who just wanted to say hi and tell Bennet they're glad he's back. Their eyes linger on me and I simply keep my lips sealed tight. *Let them talk. This old town needs its entertainment.*

"So what's your plan?"

"Well I guess I'm doing it."

"What do you mean?"

"I wanted to come back home, be with my friends again, have a moment to slow down while catching up with the life I left behind."

The way he says 'left behind' resonates and I find myself staring down at the small pool of red liquid left in my glass.

"You want to get out of here?"

I sip the last of my wine and make it a point to look at him, not at anybody else, even though we've felt eyes on us all night. "With everyone talking, it does have me wondering."

"Wondering what?"

I'm so excited that my breath comes short and

shallow. Bennet's still just as hot as he was at the beginning of our date. Watching him eat has only made me want him more.

"What it'd be like." I pause and put the wine glass down. "You know. If you and I… They're already saying it and I figure we might as well…"

I let the sentence trail off suggestively, and Bennet's eyes darken. He shifts in his seat. He's *clearly* feeling the same as me, clearly wants me, and I'd like to be somewhere *without* a bunch of people staring at us so I can find out what Bennet Thompson is like when he lets himself go after something he wants.

When he lets himself go after *me*.

Bennet clears his throat and sits up straight. The energy coming off him is pure desire, even here in this little restaurant with half the town watching.

He doesn't seem to notice any of them. Doesn't seem to care at all that everybody's going to talk about us for the rest of the evening.

"You want to go back to my place?"

chapter
Eight

Bennet

I CAN'T KEEP MY HANDS OFF AUBREY, AND THIS time, I don't have to.

There's no high school friend groups in the way.

No bar full of people watching and talking. There's no one but us and what we both want.

I drive her back to my place, a bachelor pad I'm renting from a friend until I get my own place. It's quiet as we drive although her hand is held tight in mine and I'm pushing the speed limit. The second we're through the front door, she's on me.

Or I'm on her.

She ends up with her legs wrapped around my waist, her back against the door, and her arms around my neck. I kiss her like I've been starved for her. She tastes sweet and moans softly, urging me on and kisses me back like she doesn't know the meaning of a *good, small-town girl.* It's the hottest kiss I've ever shared with anyone. I'm hard as a rock by the time she starts clawing at the buttons of my shirt.

I don't have time to second guess the barely furnished place. Or what she'll think of the boxes still sprawled out. Without the lights on, it's dark anyway. We bump into a few boxes and find ourselves up against the wall before I can open the bedroom door.

I've never had anybody go after my clothes like that. Aubrey bites her lip and focuses hard on getting those buttons undone. She wants my clothes *off.*

I let her work on it while I shove open the door and carry her in, then put her on her knees on the bed and let her shove my shirt off me. I've never done anything as hot as strip Bree's dress off over her head, revealing a lace bra and panty set that I want to take off with my teeth.

So I do, gently pushing her back and crawling between her legs to make my intentions known. She falls back onto my bed with a gasp. I hold the lace gently between my teeth so I don't rip it. Aubrey moans the whole time. I think she'd actually like it if I did rip a pair of panties off her, but it's our first night together. Everything's going to come out the other side in one piece, especially the lace.

We're naked inside of a minute, and she stretches herself out for me. All her curves are on display. I run my hands over every one of them. Her skin like fire under mine. Tease her nipples with the pad of my thumb. Taste them, too. I could spend hours kissing every inch of her body, but it's not long before I find my way to her hips, then between her legs.

Aubrey buries her hands in my hair and holds on while I suck and nibble and lick her with reckless abandon. Her nails dig into my shoulders as her back arches and I use her body to guide me. Her taste is sweet and with every clench and moan I know I'm close. It doesn't take her long. Her thighs tremble around my head and I fucking love it. God, it's hot. *She's* hot.

"I need you," she moans, tugging on my arms and I've never heard anything sexier. Her hair is laid out like a halo, her cheeks flushed and legs spread wide enough for me to be right where I'm wanted. And then I'm pushing in, and the words come out of my mouth without any thought or control.

"Oh, fuck, Bree, you're so tight. I just-I want—"

She kisses me in the middle of me pushing into her deeper and deeper and I can't say a damn thing.

Not that I need to say anything. She feels like fucking heaven. I pick up my pace and love how she throws her head back. I love how she grips onto me, and calls out my name as she gets closer and closer.

I fuck her like she's mine.

It's perfect. Every second of her in my bed is perfect. And just as I'm about to come, she pushes at my shoulders until I roll over. Bree rides it out on top of me, her hands planted on my chest, staring down into my eyes and my heart stutters. Just as she gets close, she slows and I can't have that. I reach up, kissing her and molding her lips to mine and roll her back over to help her find her release. I fuck her harder and faster, kissing her while she cries out my name as she finds her release with me.

As our breathing levels out, and our warm breath mingles, I slowly come back down to reality.

We didn't bother to turn any lights on, but there's a streetlight not far from my window, and her eyes sparkle in the dim light.

I rest my hands on her waist and she tucks herself into my side.

"I don't want to screw this up," I admit as I pull her close and drop a kiss to her temple.

I can feel her smiling. "I could cut to the chase for you?"

Fuck, she's stunning. Confident and beautiful and everything I've ever wanted.

I let out a huff of a laugh and reply, "I'd appreciate that."

"Okay." Aubrey pulls the sheets up to her chest "I want a relationship that's easy. I have a very small checklist. No pressure, just commitment that you aren't…" She takes a deep breath and looks at the ceiling, swallows and then looks back to me.

I push myself up on one elbow, staring down at her so she knows I'm serious. "I want a relationship… *relationship*. I want to settle down, I mean."

She smiles shyly at me and whispers, "I want that, too."

"I want to take my girl out on the town and when people stare, I want to wrap my arm around her waist and kiss her neck." I demonstrate, wrapping my arm around her waist and kissing her neck. "Right here."

"That feels good," she whispers.

"I want to be with my girl every night I can. Not just a fling but something real." There's no way in hell

I'm letting her walk out of here now. Not when my skin still tingles from how good it felt to fuck her. But it's more than that, too. Kissing her gets me just as high. It all feels perfect with Aubrey. "And wake up with her in the morning."

"Are you talking about moving in?" she jokes.

"Well, not just yet. We can take it slow." No part of me actually wants to take it slow, but I want to do right by her. That's what matters most. "As long as we get where we want to go and it's the same place. But really I was just asking if you want to stay the night tonight."

She smiles this shy smile, "That sounds like a plan and yeah I think I would." Aubrey tips her face up and kisses me, and this time, there's no rush. It's as deep and hot as it was when we first got here, but we can take our time. Kissing her feels like sparks in my chest, like the embers of a fire.

"I want to fall in love and not have my heart broken," Aubrey whispers against my lips.

God. I think I've always been in love with her. I'm already there.

"I wouldn't," I promise her, though I want to tell her that for me, it's already over. She's the one.

"One step at a time?" Aubrey questions.

"That's what I'm thinking. One step at a time." I kiss her again, slow, but this time I tease her a little bit, licking at her bottom lip and giving it a gentle bite.

"Maybe we could repeat some steps?" Aubrey's breathing heavier now. "Like…the last step was nice."

"Was it? We should do it again to make sure."

I pull her under the covers with me, and she lets out a squeal. Then we go back over every step we took, again and again, just to make sure it's perfect.

chapter
Nine

Aubrey

I WAKE UP IN THE MORNING IN A BED THAT'S not mine.

The sun's pretty high in the sky, and it comes back to me in a blink—the reason I slept so late is that we stayed up so late last night.

Me and Bennet.

Together. Tangled in the sheets. Me all over him, him all over me. The memories zing through my body with a palpable energy. I can *feel* how he was last night, even if he's not touching me right now.

He's *not* touching me, but the bed is warm, and I can hear him breathing. I close my eyes and savor the heat of him on the mattress next to me. This is how I wished it could be when I woke up yesterday, and now it is.

I almost want to go back to sleep for a few minutes so I can wake up next to him all over again.

Almost.

I roll over and find Bennet watching me from his pillow, his hair sticking up in all directions. It's the most handsome bedhead I've ever seen. Men have it so damn easy. Just at the thought I wonder what my hair looks like and I do what I can to tame it but then I'm caught red handed.

"Morning," Bennet smiles at me.

I smile back, not able to hide my blush and then snuggle back into the sheets.

"Now I guess when the town says we hooked up, they won't be lying." Bennet's voice is low and gravelly from sleep, and I like it a *lot*. He stretches out, yawning and manages to wrap an arm around me.

"What will you say when they do?"

The corner of his mouth turns up. "That I plan on hooking up with you again tonight, and if they have opinions on it, maybe they should tell someone who cares."

That makes me laugh although he's quick to add, "or whatever you want me to tell them."

I shrug, "I don't care much to be honest. I

like the idea of maybe telling them we're a thing though," I suggest. My attempt at being casual falls flat though and a bit of nervousness comes over me as I twist my hair around my finger.

"I like the idea of saying that too."

A small smile slips into place as I think about dinner last night and how word may have gotten around. Not that it matters.

"What about Steve and Sarah?"

"It's none of my business." His face softens. "I just hope they come out of whatever they're going through alright. And knowing the two of them, they will."

"Yeah. Me too."

He reaches over and brushes a lock of hair out of my face. "They'll be alright."

"And we'll be alright," I agree.

"I think we're going to be better than alright, Bree baby."

My face goes completely hot. *Bree baby.*

"Ooh," Bennet says softly. "I love that color on you."

I laugh again, and he rolls me over onto my back and kisses me. Now it's not just my face that's hot. It's my whole body. Warmth, all down through my chest and my belly and my hips. Warmth everywhere.

He kisses me slow and deep, taking his time, letting his body rest above me in the bed. When he finally breaks the kiss, it's with a soft sound, like it's the worst thing in the world to stop.

"What time do you have to be in the office?" he asks.

"I work from home, and…" I reach down to the floor, where I dropped my phone last night. "Not for another two hours."

"Oh." His face lights up. I *love* watching his expression change that way. His eyes get brighter, and his cheeks lift, and he looks thrilled. "That's plenty of time."

Bennet starts by taking off the big T-shirt I slept in last night—one of his—then finds the hollow of my collarbone and kisses it until I'm wriggling underneath him. His lips are so soft, and I've never met a man who likes to focus on such a small part of me.

"Bennet," I breathe a little while later. "You have to—you can't just—"

"Yes, I can," he says. "But I'll stop kissing this lovely little part of you and go lower." He kisses teasingly down between my ribs, then over my belly button. "How about here?" Bennet drops another kiss to that place and glances up at me with a wicked grin.

"Lower," I beg.

"Lower," he echoes, and then his face is between my thighs again. He holds me open with both hands this time. I thought he'd been thorough last night, but he's meticulous now. There's no part of me that Bennet leaves un-kissed, licked or nibbled. My mind turns lust filled with the sensation of his tongue sliding over all the softest parts of me. He drags his tongue over my clit once, then twice, and once I've come hard on that tongue he makes me do it again.

I almost feel feverish when he stops, lifting himself to kiss my belly button again before he turns me over on the pillows and arranges himself behind me. Bennet folds his body over mine, covering me, and kisses the curve of my shoulder as he thrusts in. He fills me in a single moment and ecstasy drapes itself around me.

I'm glad for the pillows, because my legs are made of jelly and my arms are useless. Bennet curls his fingers through mine, and I grab the pillow with my other hand and hold on. He groans against the nape of my neck.

My eyes close and I revel in his embrace.

"You feel so good," I tell him, because he does, though it's hard to breathe. He's so strong, and he takes up every inch of space inside me. I meet him the best I can. Bennet curls the fingers of his other hand over my hip and holds me still, panting as he fucks me harder and harder.

I know I'm close and as my legs tremble he tells me to come and I'll be damned if I don't simply because of the rough timbre of his demand. I'm helpless beneath him as pleasure takes over and this might be the most intimate moment of my life. Bennet's just as warm above me, his weight on mine, and that heat is everywhere.

"Fuck," he says as we meet our release together, then he rolls us over onto the pillows both of our chests heaving. I move until my head is on his chest, and he wraps both arms around me. His heart beats fast but steady.

I did that to him. I did that *with* him. I made him feel that way.

I think again that this has to be a dream. It's just too good to be true.

"I don't want you to get out of bed," he says.

"I don't want to get out of bed."

"But you have to spend at least part of that two hours getting ready, don't you?"

"No," I decide instantly. "I can be late," I tell him and then kiss him again before I start thinking about the "L" word Lauren told me not to say.

chapter
Ten

Bennet

WAKING UP IN BED WITH AUBREY Peters is the best thing ever to happen to me.

That stays the same the day after she comes to my place, and the day after that, and the day after that. Sometimes we stay at her house, sometimes at mine, but we're together pretty much every night.

A few weeks goes by, and there's no big drama about me and Aubrey getting together. Yeah, a few people talk about it. There are a few comments at the bar. But mostly, the town just accepts it for what it is—a romance that's nearly a decade in the making. It doesn't really have much to do with them.

I roll over onto my back and look up at the ceiling as the early morning light slips in and the bed groans.

Aubrey's already up and she leans over and kisses my cheek. "What are you thinking about?"

I fold her under my arm and cuddle her close. She's warm all through the night. I never thought I was missing out, sleeping in my own bed with nobody else, but it turns out I was. It's a hell of a lot better with her.

"I was thinking it's lucky that this town talks."

She snorts, a cute little sound that makes me crazy about her every time I hear it. "What do you mean?"

"We got to skip a lot of little steps and get right to the good stuff."

Aubrey laughs louder. "Is that what you call sex? The good stuff?"

"Nah." I swallow down any worries and just say it, "But falling in love is the good stuff."

I knew from the minute she walked into the bar that night that I was falling for her. It took a little time to realize it for everything it was, but now that I have, I know—I've felt that all along. I've never fallen slowly for Aubrey Peters. It happened the second I saw her, and it'll never stop. Those years we spent apart were just a detour. It was time we needed to see that something was missing in our lives, and it was each other.

It was never going to be right without her.

It never *will* be right without her.

After a minute, Aubrey pushes herself up on one elbow and looks down at me, her hair falling in a wave down to my chest. She studies my face like it's one of her editing jobs. Aubrey always pays attention to the smallest details, and when she looks at me like this, I know she can see everything about me.

And she doesn't mind looking.

"Bennet Thompson," she says, a tremble in her voice. "Are you saying you love me?"

"I think I am, Aubrey Peters."

Aubrey bites down on her lip to keep herself from smiling even harder. Her cheeks flush pink. That blush on her is so gorgeous it makes my heart stop. I want a photo of this moment. Maybe a hundred of them, or a painting—something that I could keep forever so I never forget this exact shade.

Then again, I don't think I'll be able to forget. There's a certain clarity about Aubrey. Everything she does locks into my brain, and it's just like it was back in school. I can't stop thinking about her.

"Well," she says, seeming almost shy about it. "I think I might love you, too."

I push her hair back from her face and tuck it behind her ear. "I know you love me."

I'm sure of it. Aubrey Peters loves me. From the way she kisses me and the way she talks to me and the way she sleeps next to me at night, she's loved me all this time, too.

I let my hand curl around the back of her neck and run my thumb over her cheekbone, my heart picking up. I don't have a ring, and I don't have a plan. Aubrey deserves both. She deserves the entire world.

But with the way she's smiling at me now...

"You want to maybe change your name one day?"

"Oooh." She wrinkles her nose, smiling bigger. "Big steps, not baby steps there."

"I'm just asking what your timeline might look like... I'm not booking the honeymoon to Maui just yet." Because I'd marry her tomorrow, if I could. Hell, I'd marry her right now. I'd go and bang on the door of the courthouse until they opened up and declared us husband and wife. I can picture that, too, just like it's playing out in a movie. Aubrey in a white dress, me in a suit, our signatures on a sheet of paper, a last-minute ring on her finger...

That would be good enough for me. It might even

be good enough for her. I don't know, because I haven't asked her, but I'm going to, just as soon as—

"Change it to what?"

I blink back up at Aubrey, and...her face is different. She was grinning before, laughing, but now she looks serious.

"What do you mean?"

"What's your name?" Aubrey's voice is softer than before, almost like she's not right next to me, in my arms where she belongs.

"What? What's my name?" I ask her and a chill comes over me when she stares back at me with red rimmed eyes and a quivering lip.

"Bennet, tell them what your name is."

Bennet

Beep... beep... beep.

My head is more than groggy and my body more than sore as I'm slow to lift my heavy eyes. Everything swirls in my vision as I slowly move my head forward. I fall back and several hands steady me. A voice calls out telling me it's alright.

"Where am I?" I question and that's when I realize how dry my throat is. "What happened?"

Three faces I've never seen come into focus. All three in blue scrubs.

"Mister. Can you tell us your name?" the first one asks, a young brunette with wide, dark brown eyes and tan skin. She waits a moment, keeping my gaze and it's then I realize that I don't know.

I can't remember. Blinking rapidly, I look down and register that I'm in a hospital bed and wearing one of those cheap gowns. I clench my hand closed and open and reach for my leg but other nurse stops me.

She's taller than the first and looks a bit older with her blonde hair tucked back in a tight bun. "Sir please, could you tell us your name?"

Chills run down my arms and I don't know why. It's like a memory that won't come into focus.

I say the only thing I keep thinking, "Where's Bree?"

"Can you tell me who Bree is?" The first nurse asks me, calmness I'm not sure is real.

That chill comes back and my head pounds with a pain that refuses to be ignored.

But all I can focus on is her. *Bree.* "Where is she? Is she okay?"

"We can find her for you. Do you know her last name?" the third nurse asks but I don't know and fear takes a grip on me. I don't remember anything. Not my address, my own name. I don't know.

They keep asking me questions and telling me it's alright when I know it's not.

As emotions tighten my voice, I tell them the only thing I know, "I don't remember anything, but I know I need Bree."

This is not the end...
The Fall in Love Again series will feature Bennet and Bree falling in love on the small fictional street of Cedar Lane over and over again while the real world has had other plans for them. Because love is endless and this is what forever means. In any and every life, their love was meant to be. And there's so much to tell in the dreams where they get to meet again for the first time every night.

There is more to come from the
Fall in Love Again series.

about the
Author

Thank you so much for reading my romances. I'm just a stay at home mom and avid reader turned author and I couldn't be happier.

I hope you love my books as much as I do!

More by Willow Winters
www.WillowWintersWrites.com/books